The Magician's Heart

Daily Graphic

E. Nesbit

The Magician's Heart

illustrations by John Lawrence

Piccolo Pan Books London and Sydney

First published by Ernest Benn Ltd in *The Magic World* 1912
Published 1971 by Hamish Hamilton Children's Books Ltd
This edition published 1979 by Pan Books Ltd,
Cavaye Place, London SW10 9PG

ISBN 0 330 25736 6
Printed and bound in Great Britain by
Richard Clay (The Chaucer Press) Ltd, Bungay, Suffolk

WE all have our weaknesses. Mine is mulberries. Yours, perhaps, motor-cars. Professor Taykin's was christenings—royal christenings. He always expected to be asked to the christening parties of all the little royal babies, and of course he never was, because he was not a lord, or a duke, or a seller of bacon and tea, or anything really high class, but merely a wicked magician, who by economy and strict attention to customers had worked up a very good business of his own. He had not always been wicked. He was born quite good, I believe, and his old nurse, who had long since married a farmer and retired into the calm of country life, always used to say that he was the duckiest little boy in a plaid frock with the dearest little fat legs. But he had changed since he was a boy, as a good many other people do—perhaps it was his trade. I dare say you've noticed that cobblers are usually thin, and brewers are generally fat, and magicians are almost always wicked.

Well, his weakness (for christenings)

grew stronger and stronger because it was never indulged, and at last he "took the bull into his own hands," as the Irish footman at the palace said, and went to a christening without being asked. It was a very grand party given by the King of the Fortunate Islands, and the little Prince was christened Fortunatus. No one took any notice of Professor Taykin. They were too polite to turn him out, but they made him wish he'd never come. He felt quite an outsider, as indeed he was, and this made him furious. So that when all the bright, light, laughing fairy godmothers

were crowding round the blue satin cradle, and giving gifts of beauty and strength and goodness to the baby, the Magician suddenly did a very difficult charm (in his head, like you do mental arithmetic), and said:

"Young Forty may be all that, but *I* say he shall be the stupidest prince in the world," and on that he vanished in a puff of red smoke with a smell like the Fifth of November in a back garden on Streatham Hill, and as he left no address the King of the Fortunate Islands couldn't prosecute him for high treason.

Taykin was very glad to think that he had made such a lot of people unhappy —the whole court was in tears when he left, including the baby—and he looked in the papers for another royal christening, so that he could go to that and make

Daily Graphic

a lot more people miserable. And there was one fixed for the very next Wednesday. The Magician went to that too, disguised as a wealthy merchant.

This time the baby was a girl. Taykin kept close to the pink velvet cradle, and when all the nice qualities in the world had been given to the Princess he suddenly said: "Little Aura may be all that, but *I* say she shall be the ugliest princess in all the world."

And instantly she was. It was terrible. And she had been such a beautiful baby too. Everyone had been saying that she was the most beautiful baby they had ever seen. This sort of thing is often said at christenings.

Having uglified the unfortunate little Princess the Magician did the spell (in his mind, just as you do your spelling) to make himself vanish, but to his horror there was no red smoke and no smell of fireworks, and there he was, still, where he now very much wished not to be. Because one of the fairies there had seen, just one second too late to save the Princess, what he was up to, and had made a strong little charm in a great hurry to prevent his vanishing. This fairy was a White Witch, and of course

you know that White Magic is much stronger than Black Magic, as well as more suited for drawing-room performances. So there the Magician stood, "looking like a thunderstruck pig," as someone unkindly said, and the dear White Witch bent down and kissed the baby Princess.

"There!" she said, "you can keep that

kiss till you want it. When the time comes you'll know what to do with it. The Magician can't vanish, sire. You'd better arrest him."

"Arrest that person," said the King, pointing to Taykin. "I suppose your charms are of a permanent nature, madam."

"Quite," said the Fairy, "at least they never go till there's no longer any use for them."

So the Magician was shut up in an enormously high tower and allowed to play with magic; but none of his spells could act outside the tower so he was never able to pass the extra double guard that watched outside night and day. The King would have liked to have the Magician executed but the White Witch warned him that this would never do.

NO VISITORS

"Don't you see," she said, "he's the only person who can make the Princess beautiful again. And he'll do it some day. But don't you go asking him to do it. He'll never do anything to oblige you. He's that sort of man."

So the years rolled on. The Magician stayed in the tower and did magic and was very bored, for it is dull to take white rabbits out of your hat, and your hat out of nothing when there's no one to see you.

Prince Fortunatus was such a stupid little boy that he got lost quite early in the story, and went about the country saying his name was James, which it wasn't. A baker's wife found him and adopted him, and sold the diamond buttons of his little overcoat for three hundred pounds, and as she was a very honest woman she put two hundred away for James to have when he grew up.

The years rolled on. Aura continued to be hideous, and she was very unhappy, till on her twentieth birthday her married cousin Belinda came to see her. Now Belinda had been made ugly in her cradle too, so she could sympathize as no one else could.

"But *I* got out of it all right, and so will you," said Belinda. "I'm sure the first thing to do is to find a magician."

"Father banished them all twenty years ago," said Aura behind her veil, "all but the one who uglified me."

"Then I should go to *him*," said beautiful Belinda. "Dress up as a beggar maid, and give him fifty pounds to do

it. Not more, or he may suspect that you're not a beggar maid. It will be great fun. I'd go with you only I promised Bellamant faithfully that I'd be home to lunch." And off she went in her mother-of-pearl coach, leaving Aura to look through the bound volumes of *The Perfect Lady* in the palace library, to find out the proper costume for a beggar maid.

Now that very morning the Magician's old nurse had packed up a ham and some eggs and some honey and some apples and a sweet bunch of old-fashioned flowers, and borrowed

the baker's boy to hold the horse for her, and started off to see the Magician. It was forty years since she'd seen him, but she loved him still, and now she thought she could do him a good turn.

She asked in the town for his address, and learned that he lived in the Black Tower.

"But you'd best be careful," the townsfolk said, "he's a spiteful chap."

"Bless you," said the old nurse, "he won't hurt me as nursed him when he was a babe, in a plaid frock with the dearest little fat legs ever you see."

So she got to the tower, and the guards let her through. Taykin was almost pleased to see her—remember he had had no visitors for twenty years—and he was quite pleased to see the ham and the honey.

"But where did I put them *h*eggs?" said the nurse, "and the apples—I must have left them at home after all."

She had. But the Magician just waved his hand in the air, and there was a basket of apples that hadn't been there before. The eggs he took out of her bonnet, the folds of her shawl, and even from his own mouth, just like a conjuror does. Only of course he was a real Magician.

"Lor!" said she, "it's like magic."

"It *is* magic," said he. "That's my trade. It's quite a pleasure to have an audience again. I've lived here alone for twenty years. It's very lonely, especially of an evening."

"Can't you get out?" said the nurse.

"No. King's orders must be respected, but it's a dog's life." He sniffed, made himself a magic handkerchief out of empty air, and wiped his eyes.

"Take an apprentice, my dear," said the nurse.

"And teach him my magic? Not me."

"Suppose you got one so stupid he couldn't learn?"

"That would be all right—but it's no use advertising for a stupid person—you'd get no answers."

"You needn't advertise," said the nurse; and she went out and brought in James, who was really the Prince of the

Fortunate Islands, and also the baker's boy she had brought with her to hold the horse's head.

"Now, James," she said, "you'd like to be apprenticed, wouldn't you?"

"Yes," said the poor stupid boy.

"Then give the gentleman your money, James."

James did.

"My last doubts vanish," said the

Magician, "he *is* stupid. Nurse, let us celebrate the occasion with a little drop of something. Not before the boy because of setting an example. James, wash up. Not here, silly: in the back kitchen."

So James washed up, and as he was very clumsy he happened to break a little bottle of essence of dreams that was on the shelf, and instantly there floated up from the washing-up water the vision of a princess more beautiful than the day—so beautiful that even James could not help seeing how beautiful she was, and holding out his arms to her as she came floating through the air above the kitchen sink. But when he held out his arms she vanished. He sighed and washed up harder than ever.

"I wish I wasn't so stupid," he said, and then there was a knock at the door.

James wiped his hands and opened. Someone stood there in very picturesque rags and tatters. "Please," said someone, who was of course the Princess, "is Professor Taykin at home?"

"Walk in, please," said James.

"My snakes alive!" said Taykin, "what a day we're having. Three visitors in one morning. How kind of you to call. Won't you take a chair?"

"I hoped," said the veiled Princess, "that you'd give me something else to take."

"A glass of wine," said Taykin. "You'll take a glass of wine?"

"No, thank you," said the beggar maid who was the Princess.

"Then take . . . take your veil off," said the nurse, "or you won't feel the benefit of it when you go out."

"I can't," said Aura, "it wouldn't be safe."

"Too beautiful, eh?" said the Magician. "Still—you're quite safe here."

"Can you do magic?" she abruptly asked.

"A little," said he ironically.

"Well," said she, "it's like this. I'm so ugly no one can bear to look at me. And

I want to go as kitchen-maid to the palace. They want a cook and a scullion and a kitchen-maid. I thought perhaps you'd give me something to make me pretty. I'm only a poor beggar maid . . . it would be a great thing to me if . . ."

"Go along with you," said Taykin, very cross indeed. "I never give to beggars."

"Here's twopence," whispered poor James, pressing it into her hand, "it's all I've got left."

"Thank you," she whispered back. "You are good."

And to the Magician she said:

"I happen to have fifty pounds. I'll give it you for a new face."

"Done," cried Taykin. "Here's

another stupid one!" He grabbed the money, waved his wand, and then and there before the astonished eyes of the nurse and the apprentice the ugly beggar maid became the loveliest princess in the world.

"Lor!" said the nurse.

"My dream!" cried the apprentice.

"Please," said the Princess, "can I have a looking-glass?" The apprentice ran to unhook the one that hung over the kitchen sink, and handed it to her. "Oh," she said, "how *very* pretty I am. How can I thank you?"

"Quite easily," said the Magician,

"beggar maid as you are, I hereby offer you my hand and heart."

He put his hand into his waistcoat and

pulled out his heart. It was fat and pink, and the Princess did not like the look of it.

"Thank you very much," said she, "but I'd rather not."

"But I insist," said Taykin.

"But really, your offer . . ."

"Most handsome, I'm sure," said the nurse.

"My affections are engaged," said the Princess, looking down. "I can't marry you."

"Am I to take this as a refusal?" asked Taykin; and the Princess said she feared that he was.

"Very well, then," he said, "I shall see you home, and ask your father about it. He'll not let you refuse an offer like this. Nurse, come and tie my necktie."

So he went out, and the nurse with him.

Then the Princess told the apprentice in a very great hurry who she was.

"It would never do," she said, "for him to see me home. He'd find out that I was the Princess, and he'd uglify me again in no time."

"He sha'n't see you home," said James. "I may be stupid but I'm strong too."

"How brave you are," said Aura admiringly, "but I'd rather slip away quietly, without any fuss. Can't you undo the patent lock of that door?" The apprentice tried but he was too stupid, and the Princess was not strong enough.

"I'm sorry," said the apprentice who was a prince. "I can't undo the door, but when *he* does I'll hold him and you can get away. I dreamed of you this morning," he added.

"I dreamed of you too," said she, "but you were different."

"Perhaps," said poor James sadly, "the

person you dreamed about wasn't stupid, and I am."

"Are you *really*?" cried the Princess. "I *am* so glad!"

"That's rather unkind, isn't it?" said he.

"No; because if *that*'s all that makes you different from the man I dreamed about I can soon make *that* all right."

And with that she put her hands on his shoulders and kissed him. And at her kiss his stupidness passed away like a cloud, and he became as clever as any-one need be; and besides knowing all the ordinary lessons he would have learned if he had stayed at home in his palace, he knew who he was, and where he was, and why, and he knew all the geography of his father's kingdom, and the exports and imports and the conditions of politics. And he knew also that the Princess loved him.

So he caught her in his arms and kissed her, and they were very happy, and told each other over and over again what a beautiful world it was, and how wonderful it was that they should have found each other, seeing that the world is not only beautiful but rather large.

"That first one was a magic kiss, you

know," said she. "My fairy godmother gave it to me, and I've been keeping it all these years for you. You must get away from here and come to the palace. Oh, you'll manage it—you're clever now."

"Yes," he said, "I *am* clever now. I can undo the lock for you. Go, my dear, go before he comes back."

So the Princess went. And only just in time; for as she went out of one door Taykin came in at the other.

He was furious to find her gone; and I should not like to write down the things he said to his apprentice when he

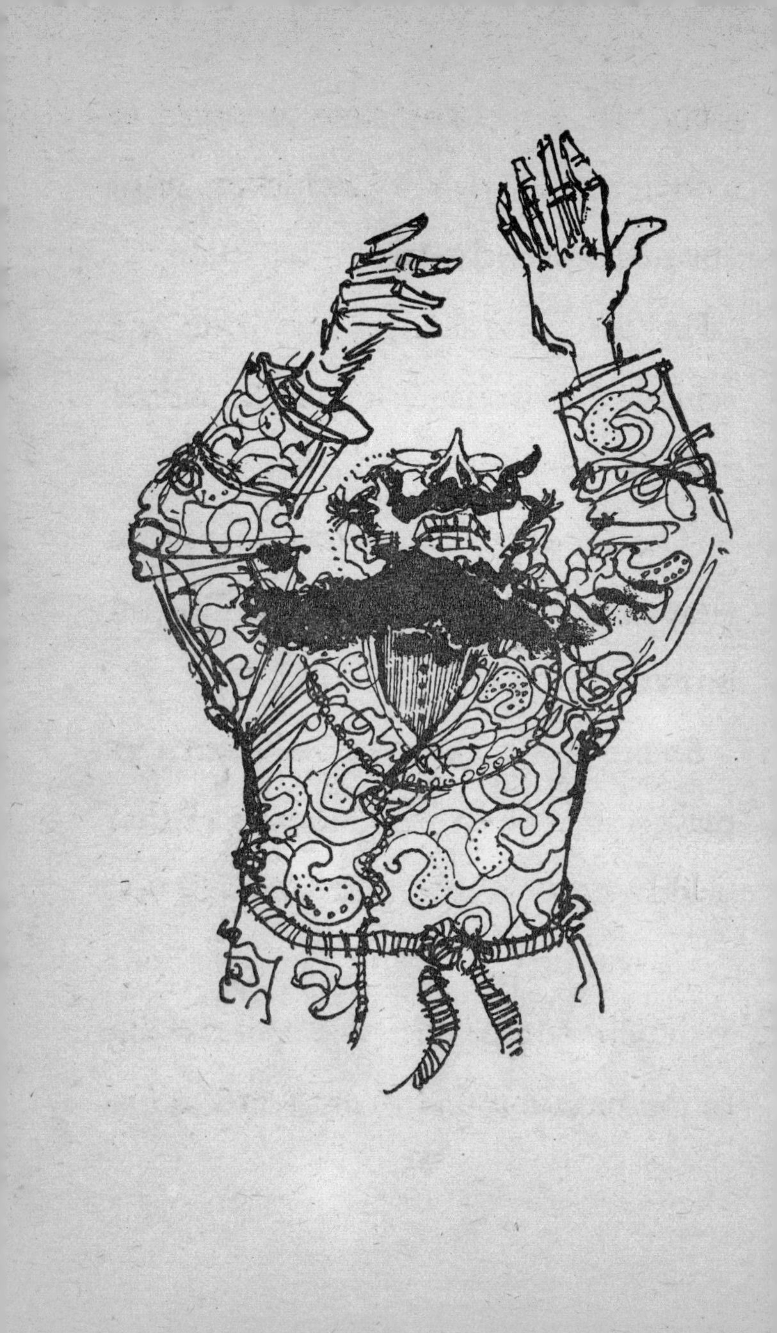

found that James had been so stupid as to open the door for her. They were not polite things at all.

He tried to follow her. But the Princess had warned the guards, and he could not get out.

"Oh," he cried, "if only my old magic would work outside this tower. I'd soon be even with her."

And then in a strange, confused, yet quite sure way, he felt that the spell that held him, the White Witch's spell, was dissolved.

"To the palace!" he cried; and rushing to the cauldron that hung over the fire

he leaped into it, leaped out in the form of a red lion, and disappeared.

Without a moment's hesitation the Prince, who was his apprentice, followed him, calling out the same words and leaping into the same cauldron,

while the poor nurse screamed and wrung her hands. As he touched the liquor in the cauldron he felt that he was not quite himself. He was, in fact, a green dragon. He felt himself vanish—a most uncomfortable sensation—and reappeared, with a suddenness that took his breath away, in his own form and at the back-door of the palace.

The time had been short, but already the Magician had succeeded in obtaining an engagement as palace cook. How he did it without references I don't know. Perhaps he made the references by magic as he had made the eggs and the apples and the handkerchief.

Taykin's astonishment and annoyance at being followed by his faithful apprentice were soon soothed, for he saw that a stupid scullion would be of great use. Of course he had no idea that

James had been made clever by a kiss.

"But how are you going to cook?" asked the apprentice. "You don't know how!"

"I shall cook," said Taykin, "as I do everything else—by magic." And he did. I wish I had time to tell you how he turned out a hot dinner of seventeen courses from totally empty saucepans, how James looked in a cupboard for spices and found it empty, and how next moment the nurse walked out of it. The Magician had been so long alone that he seemed to revel in the luxury of showing off to someone, and he leaped about from one cupboard to another, produced cats and cockatoos

out of empty jars, and made mice and rabbits disappear and reappear till

James's head was in a whirl, for all his cleverness; and the nurse, as she washed up, wept tears of pure joy at her boy's wonderful skill.

"All this excitement's bad for my

heart, though," Taykin said at last, and pulling his heart out of his chest, he put it on a shelf, and as he did so his magic note-book fell from his breast and the apprentice picked it up. Taykin did not see him do it; he was busy making the kitchen lamp fly about the room like a pigeon.

It was just then that the Princess came in, looking more lovely than ever in a simple little morning frock of white chiffon and diamonds.

"The beggar maid," said Taykin, "looking like a princess! I'll marry her just the same."

"I've come to give the orders for dinner," she said; and then she saw who it was, and gave one little cry and stood still, trembling.

"To order the dinner," said the nurse. "Then you're——"

"Yes," said Aura, "I'm the Princess."

"You're the Princess," said the Magician. "Then I'll marry you all the more. And if you say no I'll uglify you as the word leaves your lips. Oh yes—you think I've just been amusing myself over my cooking—but I've really been brewing the strongest spell in the world. Marry me—or drink——"

The Princess shuddered at these dreadful words.

"Drink, or marry me," said the Magician. "If you marry me you shall be beautiful for ever."

"Ah," said the nurse, "he's a match even for a Princess."

"I'll tell papa," said the Princess, sobbing.

"No you won't," said Taykin. "Your father will never know. If you won't marry me you shall drink this and become my scullery maid—my hideous scullery maid—and wash up for ever in the lonely tower."

He caught her by the wrist.

"Stop!" cried the apprentice who was a prince.

"Stop? *Me?* Nonsense! Pooh!" said the Magician.

"Stop, I say!" said James, who was Fortunatus. "*I've got your heart!*" He had—and he held it up in one hand, and in the other a cooking knife.

"One step nearer that lady," said he, "and in goes the knife."

The Magician positively skipped in his agony and terror.

"I say, look out!" he cried. "Be careful what you're doing. Accidents happen so easily! Suppose your foot slipped!

Then no apologies would meet the case. That's my heart you've got there. My life's bound up in it."

"I know. That's often the case with

people's hearts," said Fortunatus. "We've got you, my dear sir, on toast. My Princess, might I trouble you to call the guards."

The Magician did not dare to resist, so the guards arrested him. The nurse, though in floods of tears, managed to serve up a very good plain dinner, and after dinner the Magician was brought before the King.

Now the King, as soon as he had seen that his daughter had been made so beautiful, had caused a large number of princes to be fetched by telephone. He was anxious to get her married at once in case she turned ugly again. So before he could do justice to the Magician he had to settle which of the princes was to marry the Princess. He had chosen the Prince of the Diamond Mountains, a very nice steady young man with a

good income. But when he suggested the match to the Princess she declined it, and the Magician, who was standing at the foot of the throne steps loaded with chains, clattered forward, and said:

"Your Majesty, will you spare my life if I tell you something you don't know?"

The King, who was a very inquisitive man, said "Yes."

"Then know," said Taykin, "that the Princess won't marry your choice because she's made one of her own—my apprentice."

The Princess meant to have told her father this when she had got him alone and in a good temper. But now he was in a bad temper, and in full audience.

The apprentice was dragged in, and all the Princess's agonized pleadings only got this out of the King:

"All right. I won't hang him. He shall be best man at your wedding."

Then the King took his daughter's hand and set her in the middle of the hall, and set the Prince of the Diamond Mountains on her right and the apprentice on her left. Then he said:

"I will spare the life of this aspiring youth on your left if you'll promise never to speak to him again, and if you'll promise to marry the gentleman on your right before tea this afternoon."

The wretched Princess looked at her lover, and his lips formed the word "Promise".

So she said "I promise never to speak to the gentleman on my left and to marry the gentleman on my right

before tea today," and held out her hand to the Prince of the Diamond Mountains.

Then suddenly, in the twinkling of an

eye, the Prince of the Diamond Mountains was on her left, and her hand was held by her own Prince, who

stood at her right hand. And yet nobody seemed to have moved. It was the purest and most high-class magic.

"Dished," cried the King, "absolutely dished!"

"A mere trifle," said the apprentice modestly. "I've got Taykin's magic recipe book, as well as his heart."

"Well, we must make the best of it, I suppose," said the King crossly. "Bless you, my children."

He was less cross when it was explained to him that the apprentice was

really the Prince of the Fortunate Islands, and a much better match than the Prince of the Diamond Mountains, and he was quite in a good temper by the time the nurse threw herself in front of the throne and begged the King to

let the Magician off altogether—chiefly on the ground that when he was a baby he was the dearest little duck that ever was, in the prettiest plaid frock, with the loveliest fat legs.

The King, moved by these arguments, said:

"I'll spare him if he'll promise to be good."

"You will, ducky, won't you?" said the nurse, crying.

"No," said the Magician, "I won't; and what's more, I can't."

The Princess, who was now so happy that she wanted everyone else to be

happy too, begged her lover to make Taykin good "by magic."

"Alas, my dearest lady," said the Prince, "no one can be made good by magic. I could take the badness out of him—there's an excellent recipe in this note-book—but if I did that there'd be so very little left."

"Every little helps," said the nurse wildly.

Prince Fortunatus, who was James, who was the apprentice, studied the book for a few moments, and then said a few words in a language no one present had ever heard before.

And as he spoke the wicked Magician began to tremble and shrink.

"Oh, my boy—be good! Promise you'll be good," cried the nurse, still in tears.

The Magician seemed to be shrinking inside his clothes. He grew smaller and smaller. The nurse caught him in her arms, and still he grew less and less, till she seemed to be holding nothing but a bundle of clothes. Then with a cry of love and triumph she tore the Magician's clothes away and held up a chubby baby boy, with the very plaid frock and fat legs she had so often and so lovingly described.

"I said there wouldn't be much of him when his badness was out," said the Prince Fortunatus.

"I will be good; oh, I will," said the

baby boy that had been the Magician.

"I'll see to that," said the nurse. And so the story ends with love and a wedding, and showers of white roses.

Catherine Cookson
Go Tell It to Mrs Golightly 70p

Despite everything, Bella was a brave and cheerful girl. Her father was a drunk, disowned by the family, and she had had to learn to live with her sightless eyes. Sometimes she must have thought that Mrs Golightly was the only friend she had in the world – even when everyone said that the old woman was a figment of Bella's imagination; but she was going to need Mrs Golightly, especially when real danger arrived like a bolt from the blue . . .

Leon Garfield
Garfield's Apprentices Book 1 60p

The first three stories in this splendid series – re-creating the colourful life of the London streets in the eighteenth century: 'The Lamplighter's Funeral', the story of Possul, the urchin who becomes the lamplighter's apprentice; 'Mirror, Mirror', the story of Nightingale, apprenticed to a mirror frame carver and tormented by his daughter; 'Moss and Blister', the story of the skinny foundling girl hurrying to a birth in a London stable on Christmas Eve.

Garfield's Apprentices Book 2 60p

Three more stories in Leon Garfield's splendid series – re-creating the colourful life of the London streets in the eighteenth century. 'The Cloak': the story of Amos and Jeremiah, sharp-witted apprentices in the pawnbroking trade. 'The Valentine': the story of little Miss Jessop, the undertaker's daughter. 'Labour in Vain': the story of Gully, the bucklemaker's apprentice.

compiled by E. Richard Churchill

The Six-Million Dollar Cucumber 50p

A bookful of zany riddles about birds, beasts and vegetables!

What can a canary do that an elephant can't?
Take a bath in a saucer!

When is it bad luck to have a black cat cross your path?
When you're a mouse!

And what is green, has one bionic eye and fights crime?
The Six-Million Dollar Cucumber!

Pages and pages of zany and hilarious riddles – for hours of fun.

Farley Mowat

Lost in the Barrens 75p

Jamie, the orphan who lives with his trapper uncle Angus, and Awasin, the Cree Indian boy, are caught by the lure of exploring the great Arctic wastes. They join a Chipeweyan hunting party into the wild and come across a mysterious cache of relics from the distant past . . .

The Curse of the Viking Grave 75p

This thrilling adventure really began when Jamie and Awasin, the Cree Indian boy, found the strange cache of ancient relics described in *Lost in the Barrens*. With their friend, the Eskimo Peetuk, Jamie and Awasin set out into the wild north of Canada to rediscover their strange find. They come across the remains of the Vikings who reached North America centuries ago – the eerie contents of the Viking Grave . . .

Sinéad de Valera
More Irish Fairy Tales 70p

Ten more strange and wonderful stories of magical spells and emerald trees, of witches and mighty kings . . . from the land of pixies and fairies and the strangest of sorceries.

Kevin Crossley-Holland
Sea Stranger, Fire-Brother and
Earth Father 70p

Three stories of Wulf the Saxon boy and Cedd the holy man who converts him to Christianity in the dark and dangerous years of the seventh century: Wulf, lying dreaming among the ruins of the Roman fort, becomes Cedd's first convert after his sea-journey from Northumbria to the land of the East Saxons; Wulf's new life of peace and learning among the monks is envied by his own brother Oswald – then someone sets fire to the crops the monks have been growing . . . Wulf makes the dangerous journey to see his old friend when news comes that Cedd is dying of the plague.

Mollie Hunter
The Ghosts of Glencoe 70p

Amidst the thick snows of February, under the shadow of the great mountains of Glencoe, the red-coated soldiers came in the dead of night . . . They had their orders – to turn on the homes of the Macdonalds and slaughter every man, woman and child. It was one of the most infamous and brutal massacres in history. For Robert Stewart, the young red-coat officer, it meant a fearsome choice – between carrying out his orders and abandoning his military ambitions in a desperate attempt to save the doomed clansmen . . .

Geoffrey Trease
When the Drums Beat and other stories 70p

Three stories of young people who lived in the exciting times of centuries gone by: Philip and Mary, living among the Malvern Hills, waiting anxiously for news from the battlefields of the Civil War, where their father fights in Cromwell's army; Titus and Lucilla making the dangerous sea-journey from Egypt to Rome; Sam, the black slave-boy, and Sarah, living unhappily in her aunt's house in eighteenth-century Nottingham – and how they used the chance of the noisy Gosse Fair to help each other escape . . .

Nina Beachcroft
Under the Enchanter 60p

The Hearsts are an ordinary family who rent an ordinary Yorkshire farmhouse for their holiday. But soon Laura and her brother Andrew discover something very out of the ordinary . . . above the stables there lives an elderly man – the malevolent and smiling Mr Strange. Laura is wary, but Andrew likes him. Then Andrew begins to change, drifting into a weird dreamworld . . .

Well Met by Witchlight 60p

Sarah, Christopher and Lucy soon got used to having a witch for a friend. She was the nicest sort of witch, eccentric, but on the side of good causes. Her bewitching powers had been fading until the children encouraged her to take them up again . . .

Judy Blume
Then Again, Maybe I Won't 70p

Tony is thirteen and he's just moved house. Now he lives in the best part of Long Island, surrounded by luxury homes and swimming pools. Next door there's Joel who's a dab hand at shoplifting. Joel's older sister Lisa gets undressed every night with the lights on and the curtains open. Tony's mother thinks everything's swell on Long Island. She wants Tony to be just like the kids next door – or does she?

Anthony Greenbank
Camping for Young People 75p

Learn camping – the sensible, practical and safe way – with Anthony Greenbank, author of *Survival for Young People* and *Climbing for Young People*. This complete camping handbook for beginners opens the way for your own discovery of the great outdoors: experimenting in your own garden – choosing equipment – pitching tents – mistakes to watch out for – everything the young camper needs.